Planet of the Dogs

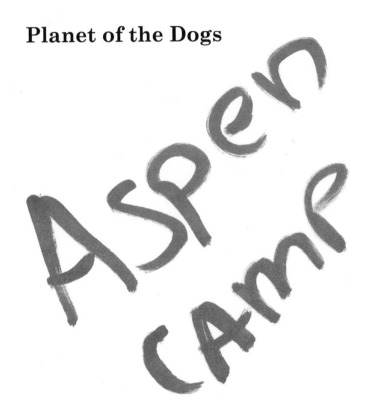

Children are howling about *Planet of the Dogs...*

"A great book. I loved it. I want to read it again."
Ned Wang, Age 10
New York, NY

"It was a great... I loved the story."
Rachel Tagle, Age 9
Alamo, California

"*Planet of the Dogs* teaches about how friendship and love can make more than just one creature happy. I love how the setting was filled with details. This tale is an OUTSTANDING story."
Heather Gans, Age 8
Fairfield, CT

"*Planet of the Dogs* is a great fantasy that dog lovers of any age will enjoy. This book shows us a better world where kindness rules."
Kyle Whelan, Age 12
Brandenton, FL

"Thrilling...imaginative with realism.
Cole Guyre, Age 10
San Francisco, CA

Planet of the Dogs

જ્જ જ્જ જ્જ જ્જ

Robert J. McCarty

Illustrated by
Stella Mustanoja McCarty

Barking Planet Productions

FIRST EDITION

Designed by Brett C McCarty

ISBN 0-9786928-0-2

To our children and grandchildren.

We would like to express our appreciation to the people who have helped to make *Planet of the Dogs* possible: Jim Lynn, for his insights and patient editorial guidance; Dawn Burrows, for her inspiration; Tuire Leppala for computer graphics; and Brett McCarty for support, guidance and layout.

Contents

Illustrations

Forward

"Like all wonderful children's stories, *Planet of the Dogs* can be read and enjoyed at different levels. When I read the story to my daughter, Caroline, we were both absorbed in the adventures of Daisy and Bean, and their canine friends, Lucy, Robbie, and Buddy and the rest of the vividly drawn characters. We looked forward to our nightly visits to Green Valley and Sun Meadows Farm, and shared our concerns about the warriors of Stone City. It was only later, when Caroline asked questions touching on broader themes such as good and evil, and love, that I knew she was taking away something more than just a fun adventure. This is an allegory whose messages are delivered with gentleness and grace. By the end, we both wanted to book the next flight to the *Planet of the Dogs*.

Charles Slack, author of *Hetty: The Genius and Madness of America's First Female Tycoon* (Ecco Press Harper Collins, 2004); *Noble Obsession* (Hyperion, 2002) and *Blue Fairways* (Henry Holt, 1999)

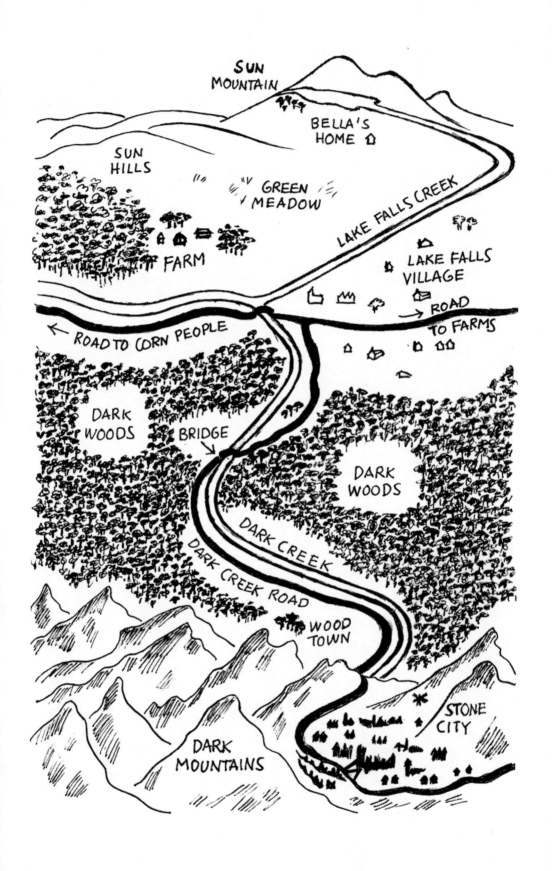

Chapter 1

❦   ❧

Planet Earth

Our story begins long, long ago, before there were dogs on Planet Earth.

There was plenty of space in those days for people to settle and grow things. Many of the places where people lived were very beautiful. There were clear lakes and cool streams with lots of fish. There were fields and woods with game to hunt. And there were rolling hills and open plains with plants growing everywhere.

Many people settled in these places of abundance and prospered. At first they had small gardens. As villages and towns continued to grow, more seeds were planted until the fertile land was often covered with corn or rice or wheat or vegetables.

Some people moved with the seasons, often taking animals with them like goats, sheep, and cattle. In other places, people lived near rivers, lakes, and the ocean where they found fish and other seafood. Others learned the ways of the wind and the tides and traveled far over water and land to trade with people in faraway lands. They traded for food or cloth or things made of clay. People helped each other and there was much happiness on Planet Earth.

And then there came a time when the abundance and happiness found on Planet Earth were threatened by people like the warrior tribes of Stone City. They had forgotten how to love. They took food, coins and beautiful objects from people and often hurt them. Their numbers began to grow and soon they were taking the homes, land, and farms where peaceful people lived.

Where once there had been harmony and friendship, there was now fear, anger, and unhappiness. Something had to be done -- but what could anybody do? No one knew it at that time, but help would come from far, far away, from the Planet of the Dogs.

Chapter 2

The Planet of the Dogs

Far out in the sky, on the other side of the sun, is the Planet of the Dogs. Dogs have always lived there in peace and happiness.

There are country dogs and city dogs. They live in places like Shepherd Hills, Poodletown, Retriever Meadows, Muttville, Hound Dog Hamlet, Biscuit Town, and Shaggy Corners.

Puppies are everywhere. From the time they are born puppies know how to play, how to eat, and how to talk with each other. And they know how to wag their tails when they are happy and excited.

Puppies and dogs have their own special way of talking to each other.

They don't use tweets and chirps like birds do. They don't use eh-eh sounds like chimps and monkeys. They don't use words like people do. People speak different languages and many times they can't understand each other at all. But dogs understand each other because they all speak dog language.

Dogs talk to each other in many ways.

They woof, bark, and howl.

They use body movement, face licking, smiling, and tail wagging.

Dogs can hear what other dogs are thinking. And they always tell the truth.

Dogs believe it is important to have lots of time to play and have fun. Dogs know how to play, anytime, any place, anywhere. Their favorite games are running, rolling, and jumping. They also like to find hidden things, explore secret places, and nuzzle their friends.

Dogs also need time to rest. They are very good at sleeping, taking naps, and waiting for someone they love.

There are no electric lights on the Planet of the Dogs. Dogs don't need lights because their noses give them a picture of things around them—even on the darkest night. Dogs always know who is nearby, even when someone may be hidden by tall grass, or bushes, or trees.

Dogs have no worries on their planet because there are no dangers there. There are no bad dogs, no hungry animals, and no mean people. There is plenty to eat, lots of time to play, and all kinds of schools for the puppies to learn interesting things about their planet and each other. It's a wonderful place to live.

The most special thing about dogs is their ability to give and receive love. They do this better than any other creature. They like to show their love. They like to rub, nuzzle, and cuddle. On the Planet of the Dogs, they even pet each other. This always brings a waggy tail and a smile.

One day, a very long time ago, Miss Merrie, queen of the dogs, and members of the dog council learned that there were problems on Earth, the Planet of the People. Something had to be done to help them.

After much discussion, and they made a decision and messenger dogs went out in all directions to announce the news: there was going to be a special meeting and all dogs were invited.

Chapter 3

∾   ∿

The Council Meeting

In Waggy Valley, on the Planet of the Dogs, dogs were coming from everywhere for the special meeting called by the dog council. This was the first time in many years that a special meeting was being held where all dogs were invited. In every direction, as far as the eye could see, the roads were filling up with dogs of all kinds—big dogs, little dogs, dogs with long shaggy hair, dogs with neat short fur.

Excitement filled the air, for all the dogs knew that something very special was going to happen. It was also an occasion to see old friends and to make new ones and happy sounds of barking, woofing, yipping, and even howling could be heard throughout Waggy Valley.

Usually, Miss Merrie spent little time doing the work of a queen, because there really wasn't much for her to do. When the road to Shaggy Corners needed repairs, the dogs all worked together and made it happen. When new puppies were born and needed extra care, there were always many volunteers eager to help feed them and give them a bath. And whenever it looked like the puppies were eating more than anyone expected, they planted more dog food trees.

On this morning, wagons filled with dog treats from the food farms had already arrived along with big bowls of fresh water. There were special play areas for the puppies and at midday, before the meeting began, the Dogtown Concert Orchestra and Chorus played several favorites, including "Woof Woof Wag Wag," "Let's Play Together," and "Moonhowl Blues." Soon every dog was wagging its tail in happiness. That's when the meeting began.

Led by Miss Merrie, the dog council came running out to the top of a low open hill at the end of the valley. The council had dogs of all ages and types so that all the dogs felt represented. They lay in a circle around their queen.

Miss Merrie was a very wise toy poodle who had lived a long time. Not since she was a puppy had there been a gathering like this. Like the other dogs, she was wagging her tail in greeting. It soon became very quiet except for the sound of the moving air created by all those wagging tails. After some welcoming woofs, Miss Merrie told the dogs why they had been asked to come to the meeting.

"There is trouble on Earth, the Planet of the People. Some people have become mean and greedy. They take things from other people and often hurt them. They need to learn again about love." A chorus of howls erupted when the dogs heard that people had forgotten about love.

And then Miss Merrie asked, "Who can help them?" She paused only for a moment before saying, "We can. Our plan is to begin with the children. They are more open to trust, love and learning new ways than adults. We will go to Planet Earth and work with the children. It is our great hope that the adults will once again open their hearts to the power of love."

Barks of agreement and the whooshing sound of thousands of waggy tails filled the air. The dogs knew they were needed, and they all decided to help.

Chapter 4

ॐ ॐ

Daisy and Bean

Daisy and Bean, a young girl and boy, were the first people from Earth to visit the Planet of the Dogs. They lived in Green Valley on a small farm near the village of Lake Falls. There, they helped their parents grow vegetables and sunflowers. Their mother, Sara, wove beautiful warm cloth that they traded for tools, jars and pots. Their father, Tomas, and his neighbors helped each other with their farm work. Daisy and Bean also helped take care of the animals, especially the sheep that their father, Tomas, took care of for both his family and several neighbors.

One cloudy day in late summer, Daisy and Bean went up into the Sun Hills looking for berries. They had filled one basket with ripe blueberries when they came to a place where the old oak trees were very high. They followed a beautiful red bird deep into the oak forest to an open place where the sun shone on a circle of blue flowers. They stopped to rest and to eat a few of the delicious berries when the light in the clearing became very dim and the sound of faraway music came through the trees. Feeling a bit sleepy, like they were floating on air, they lay down and closed their eyes as everything around them went dark.

When they opened their eyes, the clouds opened, and the warm sun returned. They felt rested and ready to go back to berry picking when, for the first time in their lives, they heard barking! Daisy and Bean had heard many unusual sounds, but never anything like this. When they sat up and looked to see where the sound was coming from, they noticed that the circle of blue flowers had changed color. They were now yellow!

Then an even more amazing thing happened. They saw their first dog!! A small white poodle came running from behind a bush, wagging her tail, jumping with joy, and barking with happiness. This was Miss Merrie's daughter Lucy. She was to be their guide, for they were now on the Planet of the Dogs. And what was about to happen to them—and later to other children from faraway places—would forever change the way people lived on Planet Earth.

Daisy and Bean found themselves laughing and talking to Lucy. They weren't frightened even for a moment by the little dog, even though they had learned to be cautious with wild animals. When Lucy rolled over onto her back, and looked up at them with a big smile, they understood that she was giving them total trust and friendship. Daisy and then Bean reached out and gently petted the little dog, who lay quietly, except for her wagging tail. As they petted Lucy, their minds filled with pictures of following her across the countryside to Waggy Valley.

Before they had time to think about it, they found themselves running after the joyous little dog, down a winding trail that passed through a forest of trees taller than any they had ever seen. They soon came out of the woods and back into the warm sunlight. They could see that the trail ahead continued across open meadow filled with yellow flowers. The wind carried a lovely smell from the flowers unlike any they had known before.

As they neared the edge of the meadow, Lucy ran ahead with a joyous burst of speed. The minds of both Daisy and Bean were now filled with pictures of two more dogs running through the yellow flowers. When they reached the top of a small hill, they saw the two dogs running to meet them. Lucy was barking with excitement, and the other dogs, Robbie and Buddy, answered with their own happy barking. It was then that the children realized that they could understand dog language. Later, back on Planet Earth, they would find that adults almost never had this talent for understanding dog talk.

When they all came together on the small hill, the dogs were wagging their tails and barking in excitement. The children knew that they were being greeted with joy and that these were their new friends. Robbie and Buddy were both bigger than Lucy, with different-colored fur and different shapes. Robbie was a sheep dog with silky black and white fur. Buddy was a big black shepherd with white fur on his chest.

The children learned from the dogs that they were going to meet the dog council and Miss Merrie, queen of the dogs. And so it was that they followed Lucy, Buddy and Robbie along a winding path to a high place overlooking Waggy Valley.

Chapter 5

A Visit to Waggy Valley

They stood together and looked out at the lovely green valley, with a wide stream of clear water running across it. Three of the dog towns could be seen from this place—Muttville, Poodletown, and Shaggy Corners—as as well as big farms filled with dog food trees and biscuit bushes. The most amazing thing for the children was knowing that all those small shapes moving around far below them were more dogs.

They went down a path and into Waggy Valley, receiving greetings from dogs of all sizes and shapes. Not long ago, they had never even heard of dogs. And, of course, they had never seen one. And now here they were in Waggy Valley, where dogs were everywhere, and all were friendly and happy to see them.

Soon, they arrived at the raised mound where the dogs held their special meetings. Miss Merrie and the dog council raised their voices in greeting, singing "Welcome to Waggy Valley." When the song ended, there were many happy yips and waggy tails of greeting. Bean and Daisy could feel the love and joy of the dogs for them and for each other. It was then that Lucy, Robbie, and Buddy took them into the center of the council next to Miss Merrie. They all sat down and listened as she explained to the children why they were there.

"For many years, we have been watching planet Earth. We do this through our dreams. We have become worried because too many people have forgotten about love. Not only does this bring unhappiness, it has led to many people becoming bad and hurting others. But we believe that we can help."

Daisy and Bean, looking out at all the dogs said, "That would be wonderful." And then, looking back at Miss Merrie, they asked, "But how?"

Miss Merrie explained, "We dogs are happy and help each other because love is the most important part of our lives. When you give love," she said, "You bring out love in others. If we come to Planet Earth, and people spend time with us, there will be fewer lonely people and more happy people."

"Will the bad people change, too?" asked Daisy.

"We won't change everyone, but with time, even many bad people will soften and become nicer," replied Miss Merrie.

All the dogs on the council barked and yipped in agreement with her. The children understood what was being said, but wondered how they might help. Miss Merrie explained. " Lucy, Robbie, and Buddy will go home with you, and with your help they'll show people the power of love. Don't worry when adults and mean children don't understand them like you do. Just by being dogs, we will touch the hearts of good people everywhere."

Rex, a big shaggy dog -- bigger than Buddy, and very old—then spoke. "You must not tell anyone about visiting the Planet of the Dogs. People won't believe you, and they'll think that you aren't telling the truth, or that it was just something you imagined. And some will become frightened and tell false stories about you. And this will interfere with our efforts to help people. You must keep your visit here a secret. Can you do that?"

"Oh, yes," said Daisy and Bean. Miss Merrie then said, "Rex and some other dogs have secretly visited Planet Earth. They went to learn. They stayed hidden the whole time they were there. They watched and listened and smelled many things, which they later shared with the council. That's when we realized that our only chance to help the people of Earth was through good children like you."

"Before you leave, we will show you more of how we live here. You have seen that we can sing and play music. And we will show you how we grow food, how we make houses, and how we heal wounds. But the dogs who come to earth won't be able to do these things in the same way, because if they did, they would scare people. What we are bringing to Planet Earth is our great power of smell, our ability to work together, our loyalty, and our greatest power of all, the power of love." A chorus of barking approval and wagging tails followed her words. There were lots of dog smiles, kisses and best wishes from all, and then the council and their queen said goodbye and ran off in different directions to return to their homes.

Lucy, Robbie and Buddy then gave the children a tour of Waggy Valley. They visited puppy schools, a dogfood tree farm, a trading post, and Lucy's home in Poodletown, where all the dogs had curly hair. And then it was time to return with the dogs to Planet Earth.

They walked together through the great fields of beautiful yellow flowers and on into the forest until they emerged once more into the open place where they first woke up and saw the circle of yellow flowers. Their baskets, now filled with berries, were waiting for them.

Following the dogs' example, they sat down and, feeling a bit sleepy, closed their eyes. Once more they heard the lovely music and the light grew dim. It seemed like only a few moments had passed when they opened their eyes and found themselves back on Planet Earth in the clearing with the circle of blue flowers. At first, they were a bit confused, wondering if their visit to the Planet of the Dogs was a dream. But then they saw the three dogs waiting for them and wagging their tails, and they knew that their adventure was really happening!

Chapter 6

❧ ❧

Return to the Sun Meadows Farm

The sky was a clear blue as the children, followed by the dogs, walked down the path to Sun Meadows and home. From the top of a rolling hill, they looked down and saw the sheep grazing. It was then that Bean and Daisy noticed that the sun hadn't moved far in the sky. This meant that very little time had passed during their visit to the Planet of the Dogs.

They pointed out their farmhouse to the dogs. It lay on the far side of Sun Meadows and looked quite small from this distance. They then sent Robbie and Buddy back to wait in the clearing. They all knew that Daisy and Bean would have to find just the right moment to reveal them—first to their parents, and then to other people. People had no knowledge of dogs and might be frightened by Robbie and Buddy. It was best to go slowly and first introduce them only to Lucy. There was little chance that anyone would be frightened by the wagging tail and big smile of the little dog with curly white hair.

Daisy and Bean's mother, Sara, was delighted by the full baskets of sweet ripe berries. They told their mother that they had a new friend who was warm and loving and would be helpful to the whole family. They called to Lucy, who was hiding outside, to come into the house. When Sara saw Lucy run inside and jump into the waiting arms of Daisy, she was amazed. When Lucy, wagging her tail, gave Daisy a kiss and then smiled and looked directly into her eyes, Sara was delighted. Soon she, too, was petting the little dog.

Everyone laughed when Lucy jumped up, and ran in a circle around the room. When Bean picked up Lucy and put her in his mother's lap, Sara smiled and agreed that this little creature, which the children said was called a dog, would be a wonderful addition to their farm. However, the final decision would only be made when Tomas, their father, returned for supper.

The children left Lucy with their mother and went outside to help clear the gardens of weeds. They were excited and pleased with their mother's reaction to Lucy. They hoped their father would feel the same way.

Chapter 7
❧ ❦
The Meeting of the Men

Tomas, the children's father, had gone to an emergency meeting in the village of Lake Falls.

The village took its name from Lake Falls Creek, a stream that came down from a cool mountain lake. It flowed past the village where it was joined by the waters of Dark Creek. From there it flowed on to the land of the Corn People.

An old trading road that came from the land of the Corn People followed the creek waters through the valley to the village of Lake Falls. Before it reached the village, the road divided, one branch following Dark Creek deep into the woods in the direction of Woodtown.

Beyond Woodtown, the Dark Mountains rose high, sometimes touching the clouds. Beyond the Dark Mountains there lived the people of Stone City. In the past, they had often hurt peaceful people, taking their things, driving good people away, and causing unhappiness. And now, travelers and traders passing through the village of Lake Falls were telling stories of new conquests by Bik, the ruthless new leader of the Stone City tribes.

After hearing these stories, Omeg, a large, strong man and the leader of the Lake Falls men, had called an emergency meeting. He believed that the time was coming soon when they would have to defend themselves against the Stone City warriors. And they had other problems to solve. They had to do something for the dry land and they had to decide what could be done about the growing danger of the bears. Every person could speak his opinion at these gatherings and it usually happened that they would then work together and find solutions to their problems.

The meeting began in harmony. They had not had much rainfall during the hot summer and some of the crops were not growing well. To solve this problem, they all agreed to start digging more ditches that would then carry water from Dark Creek to their fields. That was when people began to argue. They could not agree on what to do about the dangers presented by the bears and the Stone City warriors. This left many of the men worried, including Omeg and Tomas.

Two nights earlier, a bear had again taken a goat from a nearby farm. This was a problem for all, because they knew from Amed, who came from a land with many bears, that bears became bolder when they were successful in taking food from people. When this same thing had occurred on another farm earlier in the summer, someone had suggested that they keep a watch on their fields and animals at night. But people worked so hard during the day that they had to rest at night. Now, they were unable to agree on what to do to stop the bear. And several people believed it was more than one bear.

At this point Omeg spoke and the men stopped arguing. He said, "We must find a way to solve our problems together. Soon you can all go home and think of the best way to solve the dangers that the bears present. Someone among us will find a good way to protect us. We will then have another meeting and we will decide on what to do. But there is a much greater danger than the bears that we must prepare for -- the warriors of Stone City." Omeg stopped and looked at the concerned faces of the men.

Omeg continued, "The people of Stone City are now led by Bik, a ruthless warrior chief. After many years of peace, they are again attacking people. They have taken farms, food, and other valuables. They have destroyed villages much bigger than ours."

"Now, we know that Stone City is a long journey and requires traveling through the Dark Mountains and the Dark Woods. For years we have felt protected because of these barriers. But we are no longer safe. The tribes of Stone City like the darkness of the mountains and the woods. We must make a plan to protect ourselves." Omeg stopped again to let the men think about what he was saying.

Again, the men at the meeting were unable to decide what to do. Some even felt that they were safe because the Stone City warriors had more interest in attacking places with more wealth than Green Valley.

Omeg explained that their land and good harvests were reason enough for them to be attacked. He asked the men to return home and think about these dangers. He would ask them to meet again one day before the harvest. "Then," he said, "We must have a plan to protect ourselves or face violence and the destruction of our way of life. We must find a way to turn back the warriors of Stone City."

Thinking of this danger on his way home caused Tomas to worry about his family and their future.

Chapter 8
❧   ❧
Lucy Gives a Warning

At supper, Tomas was very serious as he told his family about the bear attacks and the dangers they might soon be facing from the warriors of Stone City. "We must all be very alert and very careful," he said. "If you see any strangers, come and tell me at once. I don't want to frighten you, but people from Stone City can be very dangerous."

Daisy, Bean and Sara saw that this was not a good time to try and present him with the idea of accepting a new creature—a dog—into his house. He probably wouldn't see the value of having a cute little bundle of joy running around their home. It was after dinner that Daisy and Bean, while playing behind the barn with Lucy, told her of the problem. Lucy gave them an idea that might change Tomas's mind. When they told their mother this idea, she agreed. And so it was that the three of them went to Tomas and explained how the children had found a wonderful animal called a dog and how it could help them. But Tomas, who was thinking about what happened at the meeting, did not want to listen.

Tomas said, "I'm sorry, children, but this is not a time to be thinking about pets. These are serious times. We have to decide soon whether we can even stay in this beautiful valley because of the dangers we face."

"Please listen, Papa," said Daisy, "A dog could help us. A dog could warn us when bears are nearby."

"Enough of this talk, Daisy," said Tomas. "We should go see that our animals are safe for the night and then get some rest. We must be up early."

"Papa, excuse me, but I must speak," said Bean. "You will find this hard to believe but Daisy and I have seen it with our own eyes." He then explained that Lucy, because of her wonderful sense of smell, always knew where other animals were. It was as if she could see in the dark. Her nose could find animals or people hidden in the deep woods or buried in the snow.

Tomas doubted that this could be true; perhaps it was something the children had dreamed. But after listening to Bean, he agreed to let them bring Lucy inside. After meeting the little dog, and seeing how she made them all laugh and feel happy, he said that she could stay for the night. "But, tomorrow morning, you must take her back to the Sun Hills. This is a pretty little creature, but this is not a time for playing." The children and their mother were upset and sad, but there was little that they could do.

Late that night, when everyone was sleeping, Lucy began to bark in a way that no one had ever heard before. She ran to the children and then to the door, barking all the while. Tomas was furious. He yelled at Lucy and was running after her, ready to throw her outside, when Bean shouted, "Papa! Stop! She's trying to warn us. A bear is attacking our sheep!"

Alarmed by Bean's words, Tomas stopped. He trusted his son but found his words hard to believe. "How can you say such things?" he asked.

"Please Papa, at least come and look," pleaded Bean.

"Please, Papa, it's the truth," said Daisy.

Tomas still had great doubts, but there was something in his children's pleading and the urgent barking of the little dog that caused him to change his mind. He told Bean to come with him and ordered Daisy and Sara to stay safely inside.

It was a bright night, and when Tomas, Bean and Lucy ran outside, they could see that the sheep were running away toward the Sun Hills. When they reached the fence that Tomas and the other farmers had built to enclose the sheep and keep them safe, they saw that part of it had been torn down. Lucy, barking excitedly, ran toward the trees growing along the other side of the fence. Bean called to her to come back, for, as he explained to his father, she was chasing the bear. Hearing Bean's voice calling, Lucy returned immediately to Bean and Tomas. After watching the sheep disappear into the night, they walked back to their farm. Thomas was very upset by both the loss of the sheep and the danger of the bear. But he was also amazed and delighted by Lucy. "For such a little thing, she makes a lot of noise," he said.

When they returned to the farm, they ate some berries, milk and bread while Tomas told Sara and Daisy what they had seen at Sun Meadows. He invited Lucy, who listened to all that was said, to jump up on his lap. He thanked her, gave her some milk, and petted her while telling her that she could stay, that she was now part of their family. Then, taking Bean with him, Tomas walked to the nearby farm of their friend and neighbor, Pola. For it was the job of Pola, who had two horses, and his brother Rola, who also had two horses, to carry important messages to the people of Lake Village. Pola and Rola listened in wonder to Tomas' story of the bear's attack. They immediately rode out to tell people what had happened and, by morning, the story of the bear, the sheep, and the dog was known in every farm and shop in Green Valley.

Chapter 9

❧ ❧
The Dogs Rescue the Sheep

It was very early the next morning, and mist still covered the Sun Meadows. Farmers had already gathered to repair the fence and to look for the lost sheep. They were very upset that the bear had broken the fence and that the sheep had run away. They all wanted very much to see the dog that they had heard about, but Lucy was not there. After telling the children that she and the other dogs would find the sheep, Lucy had run off to the clearing where Robbie and Buddy waited.

Daisy and Bean told their father that Lucy had gone to the Sun Hills to get help from two more dogs. The dogs would find the sheep and bring them back. "One of the dogs will stay hidden," said Bean. "His name is Buddy. But he will help Lucy and Robbie find the sheep and drive them back here."

"Why should he stay hidden?" asked Tomas. "We would welcome him for helping us. It is amazing that such small creatures can do so much."

Daisy answered him, saying, "Buddy isn't small like Lucy, Papa. He is a very sweet dog, but he is also big and could easily frighten people when they first see him."

"Yes," said Bean, "and if they heard his deep bark, they might be frightened so much that they would want to run away." Hearing this, Tomas agreed that it was probably best for Buddy to stay out of sight until people had a chance to become used to the other two dogs. And although he said nothing more to the children about Buddy, he wondered what this larger dog would be like.

As the farmers worked to repair the fence, it was clear that many of them thought Tomas must have been dreaming about this new kind of animal he and the children called a dog. "What does this mysterious creature look like?" asked one. "Do you only see these strange creatures at night?" asked another. "Oh look," asked a third, "Isn't that a green one over there in the tree?" Tomas, although he had still had some worries about what would happen next, simply smiled and said, "Joke all you want. Soon, you will see."

Meanwhile, high in the hills, the dogs were busy finding the sheep and chasing them toward Sun Meadows. They found one large group drinking water and eating tall grass next to a small pond. Others were in small groups on a hillside. And a few were hidden under the trees. Robbie had lots of experience taking care of sheep on the Planet of the Dogs, and with Lucy and Buddy helping him, they soon had all the sheep running down from the hills toward the meadow.

Down in Sun Meadows, the fence was repaired, and the men had separated into five search groups, when they heard the barking. None of the people—except for Daisy, Bean, and Tomas—had ever heard this sound before, and many were worried. Before Tomas could explain that it was the dogs, a wonderful sight appeared. Nearly one hundred sheep came running toward them, back to the fenced-in field. Running behind them and sometimes beside them, and always guiding them, were Robbie and Lucy. The farmers stood in amazement, and then they cheered, for they had never expected to see such a wonderful sight.

As soon as the sheep were safely back in the fenced-in area, Daisy and Bean ran to the dogs and gave them big hugs. They were followed by Tomas and all the farmers, who now came over to pet them and marvel at these wonderful new creatures—dogs!

Chapter 10

✺ ✺

The Dogs Become Famous In Green Valley

The family was having a happy supper that night, when Robbie and Lucy began to bark. They told the children that a horse and rider were coming. "Papa," said Daisy, "someone is coming on a horse." Buddy, who knew he must stay out of sight and remain silent, went out to the barn. Lucy went with him so that he would not be lonely.

Soon, their friend Pola rode up to their door. Tomas was waiting for him and invited him to come in and eat supper with the family. Pola was a big, friendly man with long black hair and a thick beard. He liked being a messenger—along with his brother—for the people of Lake Falls and Green Valley. He had been with the other cheering farmers that morning when they watched in amazement as the dogs brought the sheep back to Sun Meadows.

Pola waited until after supper to tell them that Omeg, as leader of the village, was concerned by the excitement the dogs had caused with the villagers. He worried that people would be so busy talking about the dogs that they would forget about the dangers they still faced. Already, there were many versions of what had happened that morning, as people often change stories when they tell them to others. In one version, there was only one dog, but this dog took on different shapes and colors. In another version, there were as many as six dogs and they all looked like Robbie.

Hearing these confusing stories, Omeg became worried that people were so fascinated by the arrival of the dogs that they were forgetting about the dangers they faced of more bear attacks and the even greater danger of the Stone City warriors. And so it was that Omeg gave a message to Pola for Tomas. He asked that Tomas not allow the dogs to go into other parts of Green Valley. He wanted the dogs to stay near the farm. Tomas said that he would do as Omeg asked. "But," he said, "I believe that Omeg is making a big mistake, for the dogs can not only warn people when bears are nearby, they can help to drive them away."

"I respect you, Tomas," Pola said as he looked down at Robbie, "but I cannot see how such a small creature can chase away a bear."

It was time for Pola to ride on and Tomas thought of showing him Buddy so that Pola would understand his words about dogs driving

bears away. But then he decided that it might create even more confusion. "Travel safely Pola and tell Omeg I will do as he asks."

The next morning, just as daylight brightened their home, Tomas and his family had another visitor, Bella, the healer lady. Bella helped the people of Green Valley when they were having babies, or when they were sick. She had a large garden of flowers and herbs that she used when healing people. All the people in Lake Village, including Omeg, liked her and respected her. Bella had been dreaming of the dogs and understood the reason they had come to Planet Earth.

Before Bella reached the house, Robbie and Buddy, who now slept in the barn, sensed her arrival and ran up the road to greet her. The family was happy to see her and to find that she welcomed the dogs. They were surprised that Bella was so comfortable with Buddy, who lay at her feet while she sat at the table drinking a refreshing cup of mint tea. Bella had an even bigger surprise for everyone. She said, "From my dreams, I have learned that the dogs can help me in my work. I know they have the power of love and the power to help people heal," she said. Tomas and Sara looked at her in amazement. Daisy and Bean were not so surprised. Then Bella said, "I want to take the little dog to visit Delia, the sad one."

Delia lived in a small house near the Sun Hills and had lost her family. They were potters who made beautiful pots and bowls. In the spring, Delia's brother and sister had gone to Woodtown to trade, and had never returned. Omeg feared that they had met raiders from Stone City while on the Dark Road that led to Woodtown, but no one really knew what had happened to them. Delia, for the first time in her life, was now alone. Her sadness was so great that she stopped making bowls and lost her appetite for food. She was becoming weaker every day. Bella knew that although her herbs could be of some help to Delia, the love and joy that Lucy could bring would be the best treatment for her sadness. "I would like to take her with me this morning," said Bella. "She will find her own way back and return by mid-day."

Tomas was amazed at this request, but he had great respect for Bella and her wisdom. Sara and the children were excited by the idea of Lucy helping Delia to heal. And Lucy was already wagging her tail in anticipation. "We are honored by your request," said Thomas. And so it was that Bella and Lucy walked off across the Sun Fields to Delia's farm.

Chapter 11

❧ ❧

Omeg

Only a few people could understand why Omeg was so worried about the people of Stone City. The reason lay in the past. One day, many years before, when he was a boy living with his family on a farm in the valley of the Dark Mountains, he got lost while fishing with his younger brother, Barka.

It was nearly dark when they found their way home. They arrived to find their house and barn empty, and their family gone. The warriors of Stone City had come and taken away his family and everything they owned. Nothing was left. No tools, no food, and no animals.

Sad and frightened, Omeg took his brother, and left the valley of the Dark Mountains. With the help of kind people along the way, they made the journey to Lake Falls where Kapa, the blacksmith, took them into his home and raised them as his own children.

Kapa, who was also one of the pioneers of Lake Falls, taught Omeg the craft of tool making. He grew to be a strong man, respected by all for treating everyone with fairness and respect. He was very happy when he married, but his lovely young wife soon became sick and could not be cured.

After that, Omeg rarely smiled or laughed. Except when Kimmy, the beautiful daughter of his brother, Barka, came to visit. Barka had become a farmer and lived with his wife near Lake Falls Creek. They were among the growing number of people who had visited Tomas and his family to see the dogs.

Barka had told Omeg about the dogs helping at the farm, helping Bella with Delia, and making people feel happier. But Omeg would not change his mind. The dogs must stay near Sun Meadows and Thomas's farm. He feared they were already a distraction from the threat of an attack by the warriors of Stone City.

Chapter 12
❧ ❧
The Warrior Chief of Stone City

Gable, a merchant from Corn Town, had been trading in the markets of Stone City for many years. He was given safe passage because he brought good wheat and corn and, sometimes, valuable information to Stone City. As he traveled, he often saw and heard things that the warriors of Stone City found useful.

Gable stopped in Lake Falls to trade corn for wheat, to see friends, and to exchange news. On this visit, he heard stories about the dogs. Several days later, after traveling through the Dark Woods and trading in Woodtown, he arrived in Stone City.

He was loading his wagon with animal hides in the Stone City market place, when three warriors, dressed in black and green and leading a riderless horse, rode up. The leader of the group looked down at him and said, "You will follow us now to the fortress. Our chief wishes to speak with you." He pointed to the merchant who had traded with Gable. "Finish loading his wagon and bring it to the fortress." And so it was that Gable, the merchant, riding a horse with three warriors, went to the fortress of Stone City.

They rode outside the wooden walls and stone towers of the city, past the great meadow where three huge standing stones had been erected, and over the bridge that crossed the Dark River. Gable saw a black cloud of men on horseback racing across the far edge of a meadow. When he asked who they were and where they were going, he received no answer, only a hard look. Ahead lay the great stone fortress, with the Dark Mountains rising behind it. The sight of the place gave Gable cold chills.

Once inside the fortress walls, he saw hot forges where weapons and armor were being made, warriors in green and black leading prisoners in chains, and wagons of food and valuables being unloaded by servants. Above the walls flew a banner showing a green axe against a black sky, the flag of the Stone City warriors.

Gable was brought into a great hall where light came in through many small windows. He was seated at a rough wooden table where he was given cold cider, bread and fruit. Six rough-looking men were also seated around this table. No one spoke. And then Gable heard laughter. He looked up to see a tall, fierce-looking man accompanied by two young children, a girl and a boy. The six

men stood, as did Gable, until these three were seated. And then the tall man spoke. "Welcome, Gable, merchant from Corn Town. I am Bik, leader of the Stone tribe. I have called you here so that we may learn of the dogs. Tell me, what is a dog? What do they look like?"

"I can only tell you what I have heard," said Gable. "They seem to be small animals that like to be with people. I am told they do not all look the same as do sheep or pigs."

"You did not see them yourself?"

"No. They were not in the village of Lake Falls, where I do my trading and where I heard about them. They live on the farm of Tomas near the Sun Hills of Green Valley," said Gable.

"Tell me what they do. What are they good for?" asked Bik. "Why are people talking about them?"

"I heard different stories in the village and they were not all the same. Some said that they change shape and color. Others said that they do not change shape and have fur that may be one color or many colors. Pola, a farmer I respect, said that they are small, but very fast. They all seem to agree, however, that the sheep that they keep in Sun Meadow ran off after a bear destroyed part of a fence, and that the dogs found the sheep and drove them back home."

"And you heard this from many people? Enough to make you believe it is true?"

"I found it hard to believe, until I spoke to Pola. He said that some of the sheep were his and he saw them come back with his own eyes, chased by two small dogs."

"You serve us well, Gable, merchant from Corn Town. Your wagon awaits you outside. May your journeys always be safe." After Bik had dismissed Gable, he turned to the warrior who had brought him to the fortress. "You will go, Ivan, to observe the farm of Tomas in the Sun Meadows. Stay out of sight. Change your clothes and travel as a hunter, not as a Stone City warrior. Learn everything you can about these creatures—these dogs. But let no one know of your presence. We await your return."

Ivan, the warrior, left soon after, wearing clothes made from animal skins and furs. He rode his horse toward the Dark Mountains and the Dark Woods, on his way to the farm of Tomas and his family. On his way to the dogs.

Chapter 13

❧   ❧

Life with the Dogs

Children began to come every day to see the dogs. Sometimes, they came alone. At other times, a wagon filled with children would arrive. Every day, more and more people and children were opening their hearts to the dogs.

At night, when the visitors were gone, the dogs sometimes ran out barking when a fox or a badger—or perhaps even a bear—came too close to the farm. The family would follow them outside, but no one saw what the dogs were barking at. After the intruder was driven away, the dogs would return and tell the children about the animal they had chased. Tomas now believed all that Bean and Daisy told him about the dogs' ability to see at night with their noses, and he was very pleased that they were protecting the chickens, rabbits, and sheep.

Because Robbie was able to control the sheep so well, the farmers now allowed Daisy, Bean, and Robbie—and sometimes their own children—to take the sheep to faraway places in Sun Meadow where the high grass was plentiful. Lucy often went with them, making the children laugh by playing games with them like dog tag, jumping and rolling, and chase the stick.

Buddy tried to stay hidden, and when some of the farm children pointed to a black shape chasing sheep through the tall grass, Daisy asked, "Oh, do you think it could be a black sheep?" But the farm children weren't fooled. They were sure that it must be another dog. Once Bean and Daisy saw that they weren't frightened, they called for Buddy to join them and his days of hiding were over.

The little children liked to play with Buddy and he liked nothing better than to play with them. He was always patient and loving. Even when they climbed on him or pulled on his fur, Buddy never growled or became angry. And word spread quickly throughout the valley that there were now three dogs living with Tomas and his family.

On the first cold gray day of the harvest season, Daisy and Bean were walking back to the farm with the other farm children. Buddy had gone back into the hills to look for three sheep that had gone astray. Robbie and Lucy were running and barking, guiding the sheep as they always did, when Lucy stopped, smelling the air and looking into the woods. She told Daisy and Bean that a horse and rider were watching them. Bean and Daisy looked at the woods, but could see nothing. Bean remembered the warning his father had given them about strangers. "Daisy, you and Robbie take the sheep and the other children back to the fenced-in meadow," said Bean." I will follow Lucy to see this rider who hides and watches us."

Chapter 14

ᥞ   ᥗ

Bean Meets the Stone City Warrior

Daisy looked back at Bean and Lucy as she hurried to take the sheep home. She saw Lucy quietly trotting toward the woods but moving to a different area than the one where someone was hiding. She realized that Lucy was taking Bean on a path that would take them close, but keep them hidden from the horse and rider.

Ivan, the Stone City warrior, watched the children and was puzzled when the boy and the small creature, which he knew must be a dog, disappeared into the woods. He had watched in amazement as Robbie and Lucy guided the sheep, running and making sounds. None of the sheep could leave the herd and run off, because somehow one of the dogs would appear immediately and drive them back. He wanted to learn more, and he also wanted to see the third dog that he had heard about when he had stopped in Woodtown. But he did not want to be seen, and so he decided to move away from this place and get closer to Tomas's farm.

Bean and Lucy, well hidden behind a thicket of dense bushes, watched quietly as the horse and rider rode down to a place where the trail split in two directions. One branch led closer to their farm. The other led farther into the woods, eventually leading to Dark Creek and Woodtown. As soon as the horse turned down the trail to the farm, Lucy leapt up and, barking furiously, ran toward the horse and rider. Bean ran after her, shouting, "Come back, Lucy, come back."

In a matter of moments Bean was facing the horse and rider. Lucy, standing beside him but still upset, was making a low growling sound. The horse was also upset, having no idea what this fearless creature might be. Ivan quieted the horse and said, "Greetings, young man. I am a hunter and we have become lost. I wish to travel to Woodtown. Can you help me?"

Bean, although frightened by this large stranger and his horse, answered, "You must turn back and take the other branch of this trail, sir. It will take you to the Dark Woods and Woodtown."

"And what is that little creature that seems to frighten this large horse I ride?" asked Ivan.

"This creature is my dog."

"I have never seen one before. Are there more of them?"

Bean knew that this man had been spying on them, and so he answered, "Yes, there is another."

"Where do they come from?" Ivan asked.

"I couldn't say," said Bean. "You would have to ask my father."

"And what do they do besides what I see before me?" asked Ivan.

Bean wanted to give the man as little information as possible, but without the man suspecting that Bean knew him to be dangerous. "They help us take care of the sheep," replied Bean.

"Then they are very useful. That is good."

Ivan thought for a moment. He decided that more questions could make the boy suspicious. It was best to leave now before anyone else saw him. He would not worry about a simple farm boy talking about the hunter he met in the woods. He said to Bean, "I bid you good day. I must continue my journey now."

Ivan turned his horse, starting back toward the place where the trail would take him to Woodtown. As he did so, Lucy growled loudly, jumping toward the horse and back again. The horse reacted by moving quickly away from the dog and brushing against a large bush. This caused a blanket that covered the horse's back to move aside for a moment. It was then that Bean saw another blanket underneath. Woven into this one was an emblem—it was the Axe of Stone City!

Lucy continued to growl as Bean watched the horse and rider disappear into the woods. Then he turned and ran home as fast as he could.

Chapter 15

Omeg Meets the Dogs

Early the next morning, Tomas and Bean took Lucy and Buddy to the village of Lake Falls. Robbie and Daisy stayed behind to tend to the sheep. When they arrived at the giant sycamore tree that stood in the courtyard of Omeg's house, Bean told the dogs, "Omeg has never seen a dog. So, you stay here until I whistle." The dogs wagged their tails in agreement and lay down in the cool shade of the tree.

Omeg welcomed Tomas and Bean into his house and offered them tea and bread. When they were all seated, Omeg said, "There must be a special reason for you to be here and not out working in the fields."

"Bean will tell you what happened, Omeg," said Tomas. Bean then told the story of Lucy warning the children that a rider was spying on them, and how he followed her and met this man. "He was covered in a garment made of skins and furs. He had a large bow and many arrows in a leather bag that hung by his side. And he asked questions about the dogs. I told him only what I knew he had already seen. I said that there are two dogs and that they help us with the sheep."

"Was that all he asked?"

"He asked where the dogs came from and I told him he had to ask my father. I had already told him he was going the wrong way to Woodtown," said Bean.

"And what else, young Bean?" asked Omeg.

"When he turned his horse to leave, Lucy frightened the horse for a moment and the outer blanket that covered him moved. And I saw the emblem of the axe."

"Did the rider know that you saw this?"

"No, he was too busy with the horse."

Omeg turned to Tomas. "Your son has done well. Only Stone City warriors ride horses with the mark of the axe." A sad smile came over his face as spoke to Bean. "You can be proud, young Bean, but you made a dangerous decision when you went to see this man."

Bean replied, "Yes, but father had warned us and I had Lucy with me."

"I would like to see these dogs."

Tomas nodded to Bean, who then walked toward the door, saying, "We have two of them with us. The third is with the sheep." Bean opened the door and whistled. Lucy and Buddy jumped up and, wagging their tails, entered Omeg's house. Omeg's eyes opened in wonder as the dogs went to him and looked up smiling. And Omeg smiled back in a way that no one had seen him do for many years. It was a wonderful moment. He looked at Buddy and said, "You are a brave dog to frighten the warrior's horse, Lucy".

"Pardon me, sir!" exclaimed Bean, "Lucy is the small one."

Omeg roared with laughter, and all the others joined in. With that, Lucy jumped up on Omeg's lap and wagged her tail. Omeg looked into the eyes of Lucy and was quiet for a moment. Then he reached down and very gently touched Buddy's head. Buddy leaned his body against Omeg's legs. Everyone in the room was smiling. Finally, Omeg broke the silence, saying, "Perhaps there is hope for us after all. Can you find us more dogs?"

"I think we can, sir," said Bean.

"Good. All the people of Green Valley will gather here when the moon is full for the Harvest Festival. We will have everyone vote on this. If they agree to have more dogs, it will benefit all of us. Until that time, let us not speak to others of the Stone City warrior that Bean has seen. It will only cause confusion and fear. We have a trader in Woodtown who will warn us if he hears that the Stone City warriors are coming this way. Meanwhile, let us be hopeful until we gather here for the Harvest Festival."

Chapter 16

❧ ❧

More Life with the Dogs

Although Tomas worried about the threat from Stone City, the dogs made life on the farm easier and happier. The dogs took turns sleeping in the barn and on several nights they drove away intruders. Later, they would tell the children about what had happened. Usually, it was a raccoon trying to get to the chickens and their eggs. One night Buddy barked so loudly that a bear changed his mind about having sheep for dinner and went back into the woods. And Delia, the potter, began to recover soon after Lucy started her daily visits.

One day, Delia herself appeared at Tomas's farm with a gift, a beautiful dog bowl she had made as a way of saying thank you. Even Bella was surprised at Lucy's ability to help Delia heal so quickly. She soon had all the dogs visiting people that she was trying to help. Some were sad like Delia had been. Others were lonely, or sleepless, or frightened and unhappy. Others had been hurt in accidents. And some were just sick.

The dogs visited these people every day, alone or sometimes together. Often this was difficult for them to do. There were days when it rained, there were days when many children came to see them, and there were days where they took the sheep far from the farm. All of these things took time and kept the dogs busy. But somehow, even if they had to run all the way, the dogs always made their visits to the needy.

Bella told tell everyone she met to open their hearts to the dogs and good things would happen. People learned that the dogs were visiting the sick and unhappy, and soon they began to hear of people getting better.

It was very early in the morning, during the week before the Harvest Festival, when the dogs woke Daisy and Bean and asked them to come to the barn. Daisy and Bean had never seen all three dogs so excited at the same time. As soon as they entered the barn, Buddy woofed and said, "Last night we all had the same dream. It came from Miss Merrie on the Planet of the Dogs."

"Yes", said Robbie. "There is great danger coming from Stone City."

"Can we tell Omeg? Can we get more dogs to help us?" asked Bean.

"Daisy and I must go back to meet with Miss Merrie and the council in Waggy Valley," said Lucy. "They have a plan to help the people of Green Valley. You can tell only that much and only to your family for now. No one else should know about this until Daisy and I return. Robbie and Buddy will stay here with you and your family. Daisy and I must leave now for the clearing in the woods where the blue flowers grow."

Chapter 17

❧   ❧

Bik Plans to Conquer the Green Valley

When Ivan the warrior returned to Stone City, he visited a wood carver and had him carve likenesses of Lucy and Robbie. He then had curly sheep's wool glued to one and horsehide with long fur glued to the other. When finished, they looked very much like two small frozen dogs. Only then was he ready to meet with Bik, chief of all the Stone City tribes and the other warrior leaders.

Once again, Bik and the warrior chiefs sat around the rough wood table in the great hall of the Stone Fortress. Ivan told them all that had happened in his secret visit to the Sun Meadows. When he spoke of watching Robbie and Lucy herd the sheep, he took the replica of Robbie from a large sack. When he told them of his meeting with Bean, he again reached into the sack and showed them what Lucy looked like. "I felt the boy knew more than he was saying. He told me I must speak to his father to learn where the dogs come from."

When he finished talking, the men were silent, waiting for Bik, their leader, to speak. "I have a feeling that there is something important about these dogs that we do not know. There could be more of these creatures elsewhere in Green Valley. We will soon find out. Our warriors have now been successful in conquering River Town. They will return before the full moon. We will then conquer the Green Valley. They cannot stop us."

"What of Woodtown?" asked a young warrior chief.

"We will pass quickly through Woodtown on our way down the Dark Woods Trail. We will only use Woodtown for fresh food and water." Bik paused and looked at the replicas of Robbie and Lucy. "I believe we can use these dogs. We will learn where they come from and capture more of them."

"Why do we want these creatures, mighty Bik?" asked Han, the oldest warrior. "How can we use them?"

"That is something we have yet to learn," said Bik. "For now, tell no one what we have said here. Our attack will be a surprise. We will have no warriors on foot. Only on horse, so that we may strike with great speed. We will come like a sudden storm from the Dark Woods."

Bik paused for a moment and then looked at Han. " Soon, you will all possess farmlands and slaves in the Green Valley. And we will learn the mystery of the dogs."

Later that day, the warrior chief found his young son and daughter, Nik and Nikky, playing in the great hall with the replicas of Lucy and Robbie. Nik had chosen Robbie. Nikky, not yet sure how she felt about this creature, had put a child's blue hat on the replica of Lucy. "What are these animals, father?" she asked.

"They are called dogs. Would you like to have one?"

"I would," replied his son.

"What about you, Nikky?" asked Bik. "I am told that they like children and can take care of sheep."

"Then I would like one also. I like the little one best."

"Well then, you shall go with me to the Green Valley to get your dog. We shall be going very soon. But until then, until we leave, you must keep this a secret," said Bik.

"We will, father, we promise," said the children.

"And I promise that you shall each soon have a dog."

Chapter 18

❧ ❧

Daisy and Lucy Return to the Planet of the Dogs

They were both excited, the girl and her dog, as they ran once again to the secret clearing where the blue flowers grow. Daisy sat down with Lucy in her lap, and when the skies darkened and the light began to dim, she closed her eyes. Once again, just as she started to feel sleepy, she heard the music from far away. Then a soft breeze brought the lovely smell of flowers to her nose. When she opened her eyes, the clouds parted, and bright light filled the clearing. She stood up, smiling to see that the flowers had again turned to yellow. Lucy called to her and they ran together through the forest. They ran through the fields of yellow flowers and down through the hills where happy dogs of all kinds began appearing to greet them and run with them.

Daisy found she was never tired of running on the Planet of the Dogs. When they reached Waggy Valley, they were greeted by even more dogs, all of them headed for the meeting place. When they arrived at the raised mound where the meeting was to be held, the dogs sang a rousing rendition of "Welcome to Waggy Valley."

Miss Merrie came over, smiling and wagging her tail, and then all was quiet as she spoke. "We are so happy to see you again and so happy that our plan is going well. We have been watching you in our dreams and we have many dogs ready to go back with you."

"You are all so wonderful," said Daisy. "I wish all the people in Green Valley could come to this place, to see what we have seen. But I know that is impossible." In every direction, dogs of every description waited quietly and peacefully. "If only there was this much love on Earth," she sighed. "Then we would have no reason to fear the warriors of Stone City."

"We have a plan to stop them," said Miss Merrie. "As you will see, it must be a secret and a surprise. When you return, you may tell our plan only to Bean, your mother and father, Bella, and Omeg, but to no one else. Let Rex tell you about it."

Rex, the big old dog whom Daisy had met on her first visit, spoke. "My son Edgar will go with other dogs and hide in many places along the Dark Woods Trail." Edgar, a huge brown dog, almost as big as Daisy, came over and licked her arm, giving her kisses and letting her know that, despite his size and fierce appearance, he was still a loving dog. Rex continued, saying, "There will be fast dogs, big dogs, loud dogs, and clever dogs. Led by Edgar, they will frighten the horses and even some of the warriors. The horses have never heard or smelled or seen dogs before. We will stop the Stone City warriors with confusion and fear." Loud woofs and barking of approval came from the crowd.

As the dogs cheered, Petal, a pretty little dog from Muttville, with floppy ears and golden fur that almost hid her face, ran over to Daisy. Her tail was wagging so fast that Daisy could feel a breeze. Petal waited until Miss Merrie asked for quiet, and then she said, "While the other dogs are stopping the soldiers, I will be hidden near Stone City with enough dogs for all the children, the sick and the lonely."

Edgar spoke again. "When you return to your home, you will have the six fastest runners from the Biscuit Town racing contest near you. Omeg can use them to carry messages." At those words, six lean dogs ran over to Daisy and wagged their greetings.

"And hiding in the Dark Woods, at different places where they can smell and see the road as the Stone City warriors go by, will be six more fast dogs." And six more dogs, most of them bigger and stronger looking than the previous group, ran over and greeted Daisy with woofs and waggy tails. "These are the winners of the Shaggy Corners big hill race," continued Edgar. "Stormy, the fastest, will be the first to warn you. The others will follow as the invaders come closer, so that our hidden dogs and you humans will know how far the invaders have advanced."

"There's something else," said Miss Merrie. "We're sending enough dogs with you so that everyone living in Green Valley who wants their own dog can have one." This news and the joyous cheers of woofs, barks and yips startled Daisy for a moment. This was all so new and she was just a brave young farm girl.

For a moment, she still wondered if the dog's plan, even though it sounded good, could overcome the ruthless warriors of Stone City. But as she looked around at all the eager faces and waggy tails of these wonderful dogs, she decided that indeed they could overcome the evil warriors and save the people and their way of life in Green Valley. "Oh, that's wonderful," said Daisy. "Thank you so much, all of you." And then she said, in a strong, brave voice, "I'm ready if you are." At this, an even bigger howl of joy went up, one that could be heard as far away as Hound Dog Hamlet. The dogs were ready to help the people on Planet Earth.

Chapter 19

❧ ❧

Omeg Learns the Plan

That night Omeg, worried and restless, walked back to his house after visiting the village market place and listening to people who were gathering for the Harvest Festival.

Although the festival did not begin until the next day, many were already celebrating. Torches and candles put light on baskets and carts where people were selling delicious fruits and vegetables. Others were selling wooden boxes, painted bowls, and bronze tools. One man had come up to Omeg and said, "Don't be so serious, Omeg. We are having a good harvest, and no bears have attacked in a long time. It's time to celebrate. You look too gloomy for such a happy time."

"Yes," said another, "You worry too much. There has been no fighting in a long time. Stone City is far away, beyond the Dark woods. Beyond the Dark Mountains."

Omeg asked the man, "Will you join us in the village center tomorrow?"

"Yes, of course," said the man.

"Good. You can tell everyone your opinion then," said Omeg and continued on his way. He wanted people to enjoy the festival, but he knew there would be fear and confusion tomorrow when people learned that the danger was drawing closer. Just that day, his trader friend from Woodtown had come and told him that the warriors of Stone City had been seen coming through the pass in the Dark Mountains.

Omeg worried that everyone, except the men who wished to be defenders of the village, should leave the valley. He had some comfort in knowing that the dogs would give them warning before the invaders actually arrived, but in his heart he feared nothing could stop them.

Just as he reached his house, Omeg was surprised to see Tomas, driving a cart pulled by a team of horses. Tomas waved to him as he stopped in the shadows in front of Omeg's house. The cart carried Bella, Daisy, Bean, and a large, cloth-covered mound. Tomas was the first to speak. "We have important things to tell you. Will you invite us to come in?" His voice was lower than usual, almost a whisper.

"Why, of course. You are all welcome," said Omeg as he opened the door.

"We think it's best if no one sees us," said Bella. And with that she pulled away the cloth to reveal Robbie, Buddy, Edgar, and Petal. "Quickly, run inside," she said, and before Omeg realized what was happening, the dogs, followed by the people, were in his house.

Omeg sat in wonder and listened as Daisy and Bean explained the dog's plan to save Green Valley. When they finished, Tomas said, "If you agree with this plan, Omeg, the children have found the dogs to do all these things. They are all hidden and will not be seen, until they are asked for or needed. Some have already moved into the Dark Woods to warn us when the warriors approach." Edgar, the huge leader of the hidden dogs, lying down with the other dogs, made a deep-throated woof sound that startled Omeg.

"Oh, yes," said Daisy, " Edgar just reminded me that most of the very big dogs will leave here and go home after they have turned away the warriors."

There was silence in the room before Omeg spoke. "This is a wonderful plan," he said. The people here in Green Valley are not warriors. Most have had no experience fighting. And we have few weapons. But we can cut into large trees so that they are ready to fall. When the riders approach, the bravest of the men can pull the trees with a rope so that they will crash down. When we do that it will block the road and stop the horses from advancing. The warriors will have some confusion." Omeg looked directly at Edgar. "That would be the time for the dogs to appear." He stopped for a moment, then said, "I just hope that tomorrow everyone votes to have more dogs in Green Valley."

"Suppose they don't?" asked Tomas.

Omeg stood up and walked over to the dogs. The dogs, who had been sitting between Daisy and Bean, stood up and met Omeg in the middle of the room. No one spoke as Omeg petted all the dogs. Edgar was so big that he came up to Omeg's waist. Omeg then looked at Tomas and said, "If that happens, we will have to persuade them."

All four dogs gave woofs and tail wags of agreement. "You have found a great gift for us," said Omeg to Daisy and Bean. "Because of the dogs, there is hope for us all. Now let us all get some sleep. Tomorrow is almost here."

Chapter 20

❧　❧

The Harvest Festival Morning

As the sun rose in Green Valley, hundreds of dogs were waking up in the Sun Hills. Edgar had returned the night before and told them about Omeg and the Harvest Festival. Petal had gone off to visit with the hidden watchdogs who waited quietly near the Dark Woods Trail and beyond. Other dogs were finding the ancient hidden trails that led deep into the Dark Woods, past Woodtown and into the Dark Mountains. Along the way, Petal was often greeted by friends from Muttville looking for the best places for the big dogs to hide when the time came to frighten the horses of the warrior army.

Meanwhile, farmers and their families could be found on every road, trail, and pathway, from Sun Mountain to the Windy Fields, making their way to the Harvest Festival in Lake Falls Village. In the village, people were arriving to the sound of merchants' and crafts people's voices, busy trying to sell their wares. The smell of good food cooking, from vegetable stew to fruit pies, made people smile as they thought how good it would taste. The happy sounds of music by the traveling musicians from Corn Town had everyone in a festive mood.

Tomas and Sara, driving their cart with the children and their three dogs in the back, were on their way to the village. Sometimes, as they rode along in the cart, Daisy or Bean would become worried, thinking about the warriors. Each time when this happened, they would look at the loving faces of the dogs, and their fears would go away.

Meanwhile, the warriors from Stone City were having breakfast on Dark Mountain. Far in the distance was Green Valley. Bik pointed to the ribbon of blue water that descended from Sun Lake before disappearing in the trees. "Somewhere in that place," he told his children, Nik and Nikki, " I will find you each a dog."

"When will we be there, father?" asked Nikki.

"Tomorrow, in the afternoon. I will ride ahead of you, but you will be close behind in the horse cart."

"I want to see the fighting, father," said Nik.

"I don't think there will be much fighting, my son. They do not have warriors in the Green Valley. And we shall take them by surprise."

Chapter 21

☙ ❧

The Harvest Festival Afternoon

When Stormy came down to Waggy Valley and won the Shaggy Corners big hill race, he never thought it would bring him such good luck. Here he was, hidden in the bushes in the Dark Woods, on Planet Earth, with a chance to help the humans. Just thinking about helping people made his tail start to wag. He loved the girl Daisy as soon as he saw her—almost as much as he loved Petal.

He wondered if they had snow here the way they did at home. Stormy had a heavy coat of silver and gray fur and, like all the dogs in his family, liked the cold weather. He was excited to be a warning dog, and although he was lying down with his eyes closed, his nose and his ears told him of every movement on the road that he guarded.

Far away, in the village of Lake Falls, Lucy, Robbie, and Buddy followed Daisy and Bean and joined Omeg on a high platform in the center of the Harvest Festival. Already on the platform were the Corn Town musicians playing "Sunshine," a song that all the villagers knew. A large crowd of people had gathered, and many were singing and swaying with the music. Buddy lay down at Omeg's feet, a big lump of black fur with a waggy tail.

When the song ended, Omeg moved to the front of the platform to speak. "My friends," he said, "I am happy that we have this beautiful day to celebrate our harvest. These are the best crops we have ever had." The crowd cheered in happy recognition of their abundance. "And today you will all decide if you want dogs to be a part of our way of life in Green Valley. You will also decide if you want to have a dog for your own family." At this news the crowd became even more excited and many cheered again. After a moment, Omeg raised his arms to ask for quiet. The expression on his face became serious and his voice became strong as he said, "I must also be the one to warn you of a serious problem that could change our lives—the Stone City warriors. We have been warned that they are coming."

Many of the people were frightened by this news. It became very quiet for a moment. Families huddled together, waiting to hear more. Then, angry voices were heard among a large group that came from the Highlands. Their leader shouted, "You worry too much, Omeg. Someone has given you a false warning."

"I wish that were true, Tibor," said Omeg. "But you are wrong. They are coming."

"No, Omeg, "shouted Tibor. "You are wrong. Ever since these dogs appeared, you have not been thinking clearly." Shouts of approval came from other men and women from the Highlands.

Omeg shouted back, "The dogs can help us. They have already helped Delia with the sick, and found lost sheep for Tomas and his neighbors. And they can help all of us now."

"Omeg is right!" shouted Rola. Other people who agreed with Omeg raised their voices. Tibor shouted back, "You think they have magic powers. They have cast a spell on you, Omeg. We are told you believe they can see in the dark."

Before Omeg could respond, a man yelling, "Help! Help me!" rushed toward the platform. It was Omeg's brother Barka. "Kimmy and her cousin Tip are missing," he shouted. The crowd opened as he pushed closer to the platform. "They were over in the fruit trees, near Ardo's hut, and now they are gone! I can't find them anywhere."

Buddy, who had often visited Ardo, the keeper of the fruit trees, when he was sick, stood up immediately. He woofed to Bean and Daisy, "Robbie and I will find the children. Lucy will take you to us." Before Bean or Daisy could say anything, Buddy and Robbie were gone, racing through the crowd, leaping over a cart filled with pastries, and rushing across the meadow to the fruit trees. The dogs quickly found the little girls' scent near Ardo's house and followed it, rushing through the orchard of ripe fruit and disappearing into the woods in the direction of Corn Town.

Behind them, a running Omeg led a large group of searchers. Other men ran for their horses, arriving at the fruit trees ahead of those on foot. When they reached the orchard there was disagreement as to where to look. While the men argued, Lucy ran off into the woods, following the scent left by Buddy and Robbie. Seeing this, Bean called to Omeg that they should follow Lucy. Omeg called to Tibor, "Now you will see what these dogs can do. Follow us."

Tibor, challenged by Omeg, followed, but said to other Highland men who went with him, "I can't believe that little dog, or those other dogs, will find the children. But once we witness their failure,

we will prove that Omeg is under a spell, and we can vote for a new leader."

The men on horseback rode off to see if the children had gone up the Dark Woods Trail. Others, who were not convinced that the dogs would find the children, went off to see if they had gone down the old trail toward the Dark Creek bridge. And still others wandered in and out of the bushes and trees that bordered the orchard with their voices calling out the names of Kimmy and Tip.

Chapter 22

❧   ❧

The Rescue

Lucy ran deeper into the woods, following the scent of the children and the dogs. She stopped at a place where a small waterfall fell into a pretty brook. Her body became tense, as she smelled the scent of a bear. The ground was wet and she could see large paw prints.

Barking excitedly, she turned back to find Bean, Daisy, Omeg, and the others. Running hard back down the trail, she smelled their presence not far ahead. Turning a corner around the roots of a big oak tree, she saw them all, standing in a place where the trail went in several directions, arguing about which way to go. She ran closer and woofed to Daisy and Bean, telling them what she had found.

"Lucy has been following their trail. So we should keep following her," said Bean excitedly. Daisy, whispering to Omeg so that others could not hear, said, "We should be very careful. Lucy found the scent of a bear."

"Follow the dog," said Omeg as he rushed forward. Barka, Tomas, and several others ran after him, as did Tibor and the men from the Highlands. But others, not trusting the dog or the children, went off in different directions, following other branches of the trail.

Daisy and Bean were ahead of the group, leading the way, going deeper into the trees. When the trail went in two directions, they followed the sound of Lucy's excited barking. The bear had widened the path where it was narrow, and his paws had dug into the ground where it was wet. When Barka saw a broken bush the bear had run through, he shouted in fear. "Kimmy, Tip, where are you? Kimmy!" It was then that they all heard the deep angry voice of Buddy and the sharp tones of Robbie's barking mixed with Lucy's higher-pitched sound.

Omeg and the men found new energy, and started to pass Daisy and Bean. Running forward and breathing heavily as the ground continued to rise, they came to a clearing where they saw a huge black bear, surrounded by the barking dogs. And standing behind a large rock, their clothes torn, were the children. The dogs were racing toward the bear and then jumping back. The bear was furious. One of his legs had been bitten, and Buddy's fur was torn open at the shoulder. Omeg and Tibor, both carrying swords, shouted a fierce cry and ran toward the bear. Barka, Tomas and some of the others ran toward the children. The bear, seeing so many attackers, made a deep growl of anger, reared up on his hind legs, and then came crashing down in a place where Lucy was jumping and barking. For a moment, it looked like Lucy was crushed, but as the bear moved with surprising speed into the trees, Lucy ran out unhurt and barking defiantly.

Kimmy and Tip had been cut by branches and briars and were very frightened. They told of how they had gone into the woods looking for the waterfall when they saw the bear. They ran away and the bear ran after them. They came to the clearing where a big rock blocked their way. Kimmy had just climbed the big rock when the bear caught up with them. It was then that they heard the dogs barking.

The bear stopped for a moment and listened to the sound of the approaching dogs before turning back to go for the children. At that moment, the two dogs arrived at the clearing and ran at the bear. The children were afraid the dogs would be hurt, or run away, but they kept trying to bite his legs, one in the front, the other in the back, always moving, always helping each other. And then Lucy arrived, running and barking and adding to the bear's confusion. And then their human rescuers arrived.

Before they left the clearing, Tibor asked for quiet so that he could speak. "I was wrong, Omeg. These dogs are brave and clever. Perhaps we are wrong in saying there is no danger from the Stone City warriors. We will listen to you and follow you as our leader. Let us all give a cheer for these courageous dogs." The sound of their cheer was so loud that even the bear heard it, and by then he was far away.

Chapter 23

∽ ∾

Harvest Festival Evening

That evening, when the people of Green Valley went to the meadow on the outskirts of Lake Falls Village, their hearts were filled with joy. These were the families and individuals who wanted a dog of their own. And now their wish for a dog was coming true. One after another, as they formed a line and walked through the wildflowers, a dog ran to greet them, to be their friend forever. Some people carried torches, but most found the harvest moon bright enough for them to see.

Earlier, in the center of the village, they all heard the story of how Buddy, Robbie, and even little Lucy had helped save Kimmy and Tip from the bear. Every one cheered for the dogs. One loud voice shouted, "Oh, wouldn't it be wonderful to have one of those wonderful creatures?" And then came the wonderful surprise when they learned that they were all welcome to go to the meadow, where many dogs were waiting, and take a dog home with them. On hearing this, there was more cheering and much joy.

This mood of happiness continued until late in the evening and the arrival of Stormy, the big dog with silver fur who had seen the invaders and come to deliver the warning. Daisy, Bean and their mother, Sara, were sleeping at Omeg's when they were awakened by Stormy. He told the children and Lucy that the Stone City warriors were on the move and would arrive the next afternoon.

Daisy and Bean rushed to the village barn to give Stormy's news of the fast approaching Stone City warriors to Omeg. The council now supported Omeg's plan to defend Green Valley and the barn was filled with men who had joined together to defend their homes. In a corner, lying on a bed of straw, were Daisy's messenger dogs, waiting patiently for her to send them off.

Bean gave the news of the invaders to Omeg and the men. Within a few moments, the barn was empty as all the people and all the dogs ran out to do their part to warn the people and to help save Green Valley.

Omeg and the other defenders ran through the village and out to the dog meadows where many people were laughing and talking and showing each other their new dogs. The defenders told everyone to go home immediately and to be prepared to leave the next day. If the Stone City warriors could not be stopped, dog messengers would arrive at people's homes with a red cloth tied around their necks. If this happened, they were to leave immediately and go to Corn Town. If dog messengers arrived with a blue cloth, it meant the invaders had been turned back, and everyone could come to the village and celebrate.

Chapter 24

Deep In The Dark Woods

Meanwhile, at a large campsite in the Dark Woods, the warrior army from Stone City was resting. Many found it difficult to sleep, however, because their horses seemed uneasy and nervous, making worry sounds and moving around restlessly. This was because, out beyond the camp, dogs were moving around in the woods. It was part of the dogs' plan to move around just enough to disturb the horses, but not enough to frighten them into trying to break away. Occasionally, deep in the woods, one of Stormy's family would howl in a deep sad voice. This sound also disturbed the horses. It even woke up Nikki, daughter of Bik, the warrior chief. Nikki shook her brother awake, saying, "Something is bothering the horses. I don't like it."

Their father, returning to his tent, heard them talking and went in to see them. "Why are you not sleeping, my children?" he asked.

Nik replied, "We were sleeping, father, but something has frightened Nikki." At that moment, a distant howl was heard, and the horses again made sounds of being disturbed. The men who took care of the horses were now awake and walking among the horses to calm them.

"What was that sound, father? That was the sound that woke me up," said Nikki.

"Do not be afraid, my daughter. That is merely some animal in the woods." He walked over to her sleeping place and took Nikki's hand. "Nothing can hurt you when I am here. Tomorrow we will have a glorious victory over the farmers of Green Valley. And then you will both have your dogs."

Meanwhile, the woods became quiet again, and the horses were once again calm. They could not hear Edgar and hundreds of big dogs moving silently through the woods on both sides of the road and on both sides of Dark Creek. They went into hiding places where they could see the road, but they could not be seen. They would smell the approaching army and hear the noise of the many men, horses, and supply wagons long before the warriors reached them. And they would be quiet until they were given the barking signal.

Once they were all in place, the quiet was again broken with the eerie howling sound of one of Stormy's family echoing through the woods. And once again, the horses became nervous and frightened. This continued throughout the night.

Many of the biggest dogs were hidden in the area where Dark Creek Road climbed the long hill near the end of the Dark Woods. Here, just before the road opened onto the rolling growing fields of Green Valley, the defenders would take their stand to protect their homeland.

Lucy slept with Daisy that night. Meanwhile, Robbie and several dogs from his family in Shepherd Hills were taking all the sheep in the valley to the farthest point in the Highlands. If the dogs defending the Green Valley were not successful in driving back the Stone City warriors, the sheep would be safely waiting in the hills above Corn Town.

Bella had earlier put healing herbs on Buddy and his wound from the bear was healing. Now he was out in the woods, near the place where Dark Creek runs close to the road before passing under the stone bridge, showing the big dogs secret paths and hiding places where food could be brought in.

Everything was ready for the next day, a day that the people of Green Valley and beyond would talk about for many years to come. They would call it the Day of the Dogs.

Chapter 25

ᔡ   ᔢ

The Day of the Dogs

Buddy, Edgar, and Stormy, well hidden on the hill near the Dark Creek Bridge, watched in silence as the long line of horses and riders in battle dress came down the Dark Woods Road. Leading the way, riding next to the warrior carrying the banner of the green axe against a black sky, was Ivan, the warrior who had talked with Bean.

Riding close behind him was an angry Bik. As leader of this army, Bik always studied his opponents before battle, and then, with his chieftains, decided on a plan that would insure victory. He always felt confident and strong as the time for fighting drew near. Although he was certain that the farmers and craftsmen of Green Valley could not resist his army, he kept feeling that something was wrong. And this feeling was frustrating him, making him angry.

Once again, he heard that strange distant howling sound. Once again, the road narrowed and his warriors had to adjust to keep from bumping into each other. Some had tried riding in the woods, but their horses were so big and the ground was so rough that they had to go at a very slow pace. Bik wanted to be out of this forest and into the open land.

In all of their previous conquests, his army had spread out next to each other and charged their victims. Most of their victories had not required great battles. The towns and villages they attacked usually surrendered without much fighting. His warriors would follow that same tactic today of spreading out in a long line when they emerged from the Dark Woods onto open ground. But experience had taught Bik to trust his instinct, and he felt that something was wrong. The fact that he couldn't decide what it was continued to annoy him, and his anger grew with it.

At last, Ivan, riding in the lead, turned and called to him, "We will soon emerge from these woods. The road is widening ahead. Once we climb the long hill, we will come to open fields."

Bik rode up next to him, saying, "Excellent. We will follow our plan as soon as we leave this forest. Regroup into attack formation as the riders reach the open fields." Before he could say another word, a loud howling sound came from nearby in the woods. It was followed immediately by howling in every direction. The riders were forced to pull hard on the reins to control their horses. "What's going on here?" demanded Bik. At that moment huge, ancient tall trees crashed to the ground with a thunderous noise, blocking the road just ahead.

Howling, barking, and growling sounds filled the air as dogs rushed from hiding places and ran toward the warriors and their horses. More huge trees crashed down, warriors were thrown to the ground, and dogs were running and jumping everywhere. Riders were crashing into each other as they tried to control their frightened horses and retreat to a safe area.

Bik shouted to Ivan, "Take charge here. I must see to the safety of my children." With great skill, he turned his horse to search for Nik and Nikki, who were further back, riding in a horse drawn cart. As he struggled to go back up the road through the confusion of riders, supply wagons, and barking, growling, running dogs, Bik's anger turned to fear. Not for himself, but for his children.

Meanwhile, Ivan, now carrying the banner of Stone City, was trying to organize the warriors near him. Being an excellent horseman, he was able to control his horse, despite the loud howls and crashing trees, until Lucy ran out from the woods and, barking wildly, ran at his horse. Seeing this fierce little creature again caused his horse to rear up in the air, nearly throwing Ivan to the ground. Before Ivan could regain control, four huge mountain dogs ran up to support Lucy's attack. Ivan's horse, turning in panic, dodging dogs and other horses, ran back up the road in the direction of the Dark Mountains.

The confusion and fear became more intense when clouds covered the sun and the sky darkened. It became more difficult to see on the Dark Woods Road. Bik, trying to make his way back, saw Han, the older warrior chieftain, who shouted, "Call the retreat, Bic. We must go back. We should not be here."

Bic, seeing his warriors and their frightened horses, with dogs running at them from every direction, crashing into each other and unable to fight these fast-moving enemies, shouted his agreement. He was nearly knocked off his horse by a runaway stallion as he reached in his riding pack and took out the great bullhorn. Raising it to the tree branches overhead, he blew the sound of retreat.

Farther back and ahead, the sound of retreat was echoed by other chieftains. The dogs were everywhere, continuing to nip at the horses' heels and jump up on their flanks as the warriors struggled to turn their horses and go back. Bic, riding hard, shouted, "Out of my way! Out of my way!" as he continued his running search for his children.

As he approached the Dark Creek bridge he saw a terrible sight. A riderless horse, fearful and out of control, crashed into the open cart carrying his children. The wagon, pushed past the edge of the bridge, was falling into the cold waters of Dark Creek.

Bik cried out in fear as the children fell into the rushing stream. He knew they couldn't swim. He reached the bridge in time to see his children clinging to the edge of the sinking wagon. Meanwhile, Buddy and Stormy jumped into the river and began swimming toward them.

Bic leaped off the bridge and down onto the embankment. Twisting his ankle as he fell on the wet surface, he ignored the pain and struggled to his feet. He feared the worst when he looked up and saw no sign of his children. "No," he cried out in sorrow. "Not the children."

It was then that he saw, emerging from the darkness under the bridge, two large dogs, and clinging to their fur, his children. Confused, and fearful of these large creatures, he tried to draw his sword. From behind him, a strong, quiet voice said, "You don't need the weapon. The dogs have saved your children."

Bik, turning quickly, saw armed men, led by Omeg and Tibor. Surrounding the men were Edgar and several large dogs. "We don't want to fight with you," continued Omeg. "We want peace."

"He is right, father," shouted Nik from the water's edge. "The dogs saved us from drowning."

Bik turned to see his son being pulled from the water by Stormy, the large silver dog. Next to him was Nikki, climbing off of Buddy and giving him a big hug, as she said, "They like us, father. They want to be our friends."

Hearing those words, Bik drove his sword into the earth, shouting, "Then let there be peace." And he ran to embrace his children. "Hurray," shouted Omeg and the men with him, while all the dogs barked in glee.

At that moment, peace and abundance returned to the people of Green Valley. And a new way of life began for the people and warriors of Stone City. It was a day truly named—the Day of the Dogs.

Chapter 26

ॐ   ॐ

The Celebrations

Once peace was declared, messenger dogs ran through the valley with blue cloths tied around their necks notifying everyone that the danger was gone. And the next morning, before sunrise, Robbie and his cousins began returning to their owners all the sheep they had hidden in the Highlands.

By afternoon, nearly everyone had traveled to the village to celebrate. Those who were too old or too sick to travel now had dogs to give them love and keep them from being lonely. Bella, with help from Daisy and Bean, was busy for a long time placing healing medicine on dogs who had been hurt in the Dark Woods.

Men with teams of oxen cleared the road in the woods. They then moved the base of a large tree to the dog field where Amed, from the land of many bears, began to carve a big statue of Lucy, Robbie, and Buddy. He was joined by the people of the valley and their new dogs. Leading everyone were the Corn City musicians, playing joyous songs. Omeg, holding Kimmy, was laughing and smiling, especially when Tibor and the Highlands men and women began to dance and celebrate the Day of the Dogs.

On the next afternoon, the Stone City warrior army returned home. Led by Bik, they entered the gates of Stone City with their banner held high. Directly behind Bik was a black and green wagon carrying Nik and Nikki with their new dogs. Nikki's dog was Buddy's cousin Billy, and Nik's dog was Stormy. Behind them was the army of horses, riders, and supply wagons.

The townspeople and the warriors were silent as Bik climbed the stairs to the speaker's tower above the great square. He was followed by his children and their dogs. No one knew what might happen next. This was the first time that the warriors had returned home without a victory. Many were frightened. Bik looked out at the huge crowd with a stern face, and then, in a deep voice, he spoke. "We return home from an amazing adventure. No one has died in battle or been seriously hurt. We return with the beginnings of a new and better way of life." He pointed to Billy and Stormy. "These are dogs. The silver dog and another saved my children's lives. Other brave dogs confused our warriors and stopped our advance."

"From now on, dogs will be our friends. They will help to protect us. And the warriors of Stone City will become the defenders of all our neighbors." At these words, everyone cheered, for ordinary people and warriors alike had become tired of war and cruelty.

Hidden outside the city gate in a tall grassy field and waiting were Petal and hundreds of dogs. They were waiting for Bik's signal to come and join the people.

Bik signaled for silence and continued. "How many families here would like to have their own dog to protect their homes, help with the animals, and make them happier? How many would like to have a dog right now?" At first only a few raised their voices, but then more and more joined in until the chant of, "Yes, yes, yes," filled the square. It was then that Bik raised the bullhorn to his mouth and sounded a long note, a different sound from any that they had heard before.

Moments later, Petal, followed by hundreds of dogs, ran into the square. Most of them were of small or medium size. They had long fur and short. They were brown, gold, black, and white. All were happy and wagging their tails. By sundown, Stone City was a happy place. It had changed forever.

Perhaps the biggest, happiest celebration took place on the Planet of the Dogs when Daisy, Bean, and the victorious dogs returned to Waggy Valley. Families were there to welcome home their brave sons and daughters who had turned back the Stone City warriors.

"Then they are useful. That is good. In appreciation for the wonderful success they had created, and to honor those who had stayed on Earth, the great dog choir joined Miss Merrie and the council in singing "The Land of Happy Wagging." The song was so beautiful it brought tears to the eyes of both Daisy and Bean.

Before returning home, they were shown the new play land for puppies. It was started to help the puppies understand people better and prepare them for life on Planet Earth.

Lucy, Robbie, and Buddy returned to Green Valley to live forever with Daisy and Bean.

If you are ever in Green Valley, look for the statue of those three wonderful dogs in the field. People say it's a miracle that it's still there after all these years. And some say that if you stand and look at it for a while, you might even hear the sound of Lucy barking from far, far away.

～　～　～　～

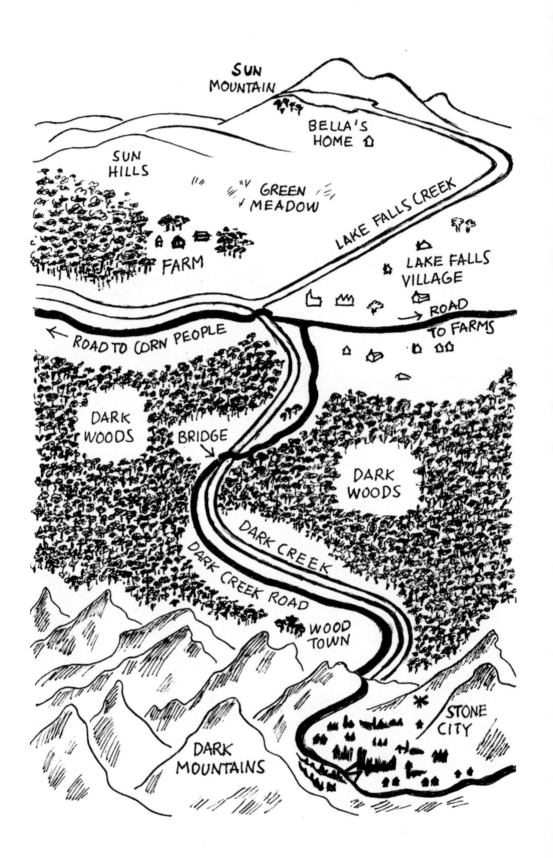

Robert J McCarty is a former Adjunct Professor at Teachers College, Columbia University and a former Instructor at the School of Visual Arts, New York City. He has written, produced, and directed documentary, educational, and industrial videos and films on a wide variety of subject matter ranging from teenage lifestyles to race relations, and from clinical computing to oceanography. His short film, *Rooftops of New York*, was nominated for an Academy Award®.

Planet of the Dogs is his first children's book, inspired by the many stories made up for his four children and five grandchildren. He is a graduate of Princeton University.

Stella Mustanoja McCarty, who teaches painting and drawing workshops, for both adults and children, at the Vantaa, Finland, Art School, illustrated the book. She graduated with a major in painting from the Art Academy in Helsinki; she also has degrees from the University of Helsinki in Education and Sociology and Social Policy.

Planet of the Dogs is the first children's book she has illustrated. In the past, she illustrated a quarterly magazine for children and young people in Finland. And for many years, she has created imaginative drawings for her daughter, niece and nephew.

Stella and Robert have both been honored to be the human companions for several dogs.